Life is a Poem

Reflections on Love, Spirituality, and Other Life Experiences

Mary Minjeur

Ordering Information:

For orders and inquiries, please contact:
1-888-375-9818
www.toplinkpublishing.com
bookorder@toplinkpublishing.com

Printed in the United States of America

Dedication ......

With all my love and God's grace
I dedicate this lifelong work
To all who have been a part of it,
But especially to my husband, Carel.

The journey is not over,
But the travel along the way
Has been magnificent.

Mary

Contents

HEALING

A NEW LIFE AND LOVE

EVENTS ALONG THE WAY

SPIRITUAL REFLECTIONS

HAIKU HARVEST AND REFLECTIONS IN POETRY

REMEMBERING TIM

WINTERTIME WOES

The Early Years

Accolades to Mom

Of her infinitesimal seed I came to be,
Even before she dreamt or thought.
I lived for a time in a simple home,
Near a grotto that held her precious throb.

The day came when her confinement ceased,
And intricate patterns of genes she bore.
Amidst visions of God in a twilight sleep,
I then became her monument to life.

Nurtured I sustained her gift—my life,
Growing on her mother's love.
Behold! One day I knew her face,
And promptly gave my first love smile.

Now what tribute or gift can I give?
What worth is there for the priceless?
Ah! If I'm half her goodness reflected,
What other accolade can there be!

Noble woman, you've tasted life bittersweet,
And God smiles upon those He loves.
For surely to give life is a miracle, but to
Grant one's own life is immortal.

Awesome Woman!

Goodbye, my childhood sweetheart—
You were the first to break my heart.

Goodbye, my love in passing,
You were at the railroad crossing.

Goodbye, my boastful acquaintance;
Your cowardice is only surpassed by mine.

Goodbye, my autocratic challenge,
You were the avenue to forget.

Goodbye, my confidante;
Our misery was our company.

Goodbye, my silent admirer;
Wanderers—you and I were too alike.

Goodbye, my learned healer,
You tutored me in a new morality.

Goodbye, my lifetime promise;
You probably knew me best.

Goodbye, all my many suitors,
You each had an eccentricity to share.

Behold the awesome woman who evolved,
Me.

Glorious Butterfly

Spread opulent wings, Oh Monarch Glory
Glimmer and glide in the morning sun.
Shadow each petal with your captive spell,
And invite the flower's nectar sweet.

Keep alive this world of beauty
Planting seeds for lives unlived.
Ah! To pinch your wings and hold you still!
Aye, but not to have you anyway.

As life ---lived, but oft lacking rapture.
Such is the realm of the butterfly,
Precariously flitting, unaware,
Hovering as the Great One intends.

The Masterpiece

Feel the matter, flesh and bone
Body recreating, cell for cell,
Adding up the years to "aged."

Heart that beats, "tup, tup, tup, tup"
Pumping life in lumps of clay,
Rhythmic song to blush the cheek.

Bellows that breathe the earthy air,
From the baby's first triumphant cry
To tired sigh of Grandma's sleep.

Timothy, To Honor God

In Memory of Timothy 7-25-04

My son, my beloved chosen son…
born of another's love you came to me.
How well I recall the joyous day when you were mine.
Cavernous blue eyes and prominent
cheeks—a beautiful boy!

You studied my face, photographing my image as well.
In wonderment I thought, "What a miracle you are!"
Moments of contentment were at day's end,
When lulled in my arms you fell asleep—
joys a mother knows then!

Standing o'er you I watched in silent adoration,
seeing your cherub smile,
sleeping soundly, dreaming with the angels.
I planted kisses and sometimes tears
on your cheeks and brow.

Then you grew and became my avid helper.
Little chores were done with rewarding fun.
And the times when 'round my neck you hung,
arms wrapped so tight,
Kissing my cheek and saying
"I love you, Mom." was the best of all.

Yes, Tim, you fulfilled and complemented my life.
Then grown up you left home and made your way.
I prayed you'd go with God and all my love,
I hoped you'd live your life as you bore your name,
Timothy—to honor God.

Winter Sunshine

Snowflakes, come down, lace the frozen ground.
Lightly, softly, rhythmic, silent sound.

Whiteness, brightness, sunlight in the gloom,
Winter sunshine, smiles in solemn doom.

Peaceful, restful, God's not far away,
Hover, snow clouds, slumber while I pray.

Heartbreak

The Abyss

The black hole of a heart—an abyss like a vacuum,
Life's blood swirling down until it becomes
A torrent of rushing nothingness.

Grief claims the nights, and sorrow robs the days.
And life is duped by sins and tragedies—
Wasted by omissions and transgressions.

Laughter no longer parts the lips; no song lays upon
The tongue. Fingers are numb to the lyre and the
Soul longs to live and love again.

What tormentor rules life—what creature
Leaps for the warble in the throat?
Asea and tempest tossed, the words snuff out the lamp.

Yet the spirit is pulled from the undertow,
And rising up survives the doom,
Though breath is nil and weeping torrent.

The bleak, vast despair lingers, and roads go awry,
Hovering like fog beguiling the compass home.
Yea, despite paths that end, life still throbs a new tomorrow.

Chiseled Love

On requited love

All mementos packed away,
Unsigned cards and photos,
Lest dreams hurt too much,
"Out of sight, out of mind."

Still one verse the heart knows.
It speaks of lovers long ago.
How time has spanned the
Awesome gap of chiseled love!

Chip, chip—chip, chip,
The hammered pieces flew,
Lonely nights and empty days
Betrayed, abandoned, loathed.

Now the hour rests at dusk.
Day's end—love's end.
Sad, but surely o'er—since
The passion turned to scorn.

A Fragile Thing Called Happiness

The trees in the glen are almost barren now,
Bereft of all their life.
Somehow I've forgotten it, my Love—
Recollections of my beginnings.
They are gone like your transient apparition
In my dreams nevermore to reappear.
Now autumn gathers to itself its ample harvest,
And fills my life with abundant memories.

A sad farewell I sigh to the haven of my birth.
Dutifully the icy cold chokes the last
Rays of the sunlight on the spot where I lived.
It is culminated: The rhythm has seen
The season change times four—a year is past.
The death of this mortal valley is the death
Of what once was my salvation,
A fragile thing called happiness.

Love's Dwelling Place

I once had a finely crafted edifice.
A palace where love beamed its song.
Hearts throbbed like jewels in a gold watch,
And joy chimed like London's clock.

Now, as rows of houses for sale—
Void of man's flesh and smell,
The tower lacks the warmth of living,
And surely the certainty of life.

When, my friend, oh when was it razed?
Why did the wrecking ball begin?
Await, now, the carpenter's hand,
To rebuild love's dwelling place.

Rumble on Thunder

Rumble on, oh thunder! What omnificent power you possess!
Grumbling and testing courage and strength.
Spectacular clouds mount in a sky of blackened ash,
Striking with awful cleave what need be mend.

Bring the wind to wipe away the barren earth of its dust.
How laden it is with fear, contempt, and uncertainty!
Driving rain pours down like accolades that laud an altar,
Soundly reminding of terror that snares souls within.

What infinite desolation you wrought, oh stormy weather!
Draw into thy womb, oh sinister bearer of sorrow!
Taking refuge from torrents tearing at threads of sanity,
Filling the valley of longing with a deluge of despair.

Bitterly scream to the boom, "Exploited!" Vulnerable to deceit.
Each woe is cemented to the first before it, ad infinatum,
Carrying the rock of despondence—a wary abode,
Where self-pity breathes and exists in everlasting doom!

Silence!

Oh swollen mouth, speak thy piece,
Wherewith you shall have debate.
Defend, defile, deface the smile,
Cut it down to a somber square.

Rich in humor, bah! Be still!
Mere friendly laughs to brighten days.
What greatness has been accomplished
By thy generous communication?

Swallow, suck in this abuse,
Say, clown, no more of it!
Silence the songbird's twitter tune,
And crush the warbling hum.

Quiver in the sight of scorn,
Cry with bitter bleat.
Tight-lipped you can force no sound,
No words to retort, only "why?"

Published in the 2007 anthology of
The International Who's Who in Poetry

Searching for Happiness

The Enemy of Love

Time is the enemy of love,
The thief that steals golden hours.
Understanding why lovers are oblivious
To days and nights and years.
Perhaps love can only be measured
In joys, and sighs, and tears.

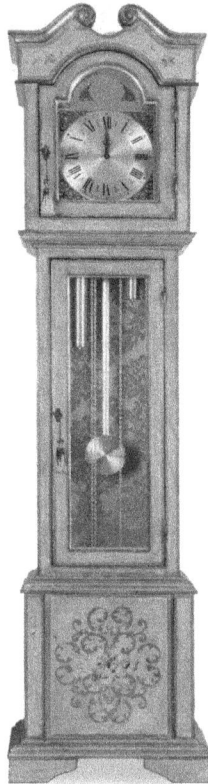

The Infamous Ride

On Requited Love

The inevitable time...
the wee hours of the night.
Naught can hear cries of woe
in the infamous prison.
Alone feeling sacrilege and
desecration, bearing all,
As life and death
throb simultaneously.

Oddly, they beckon and pulsate
in harmonious rhythm,
While amulets of tears fall
to the tune of a wicked stick.
Surely, dawn finds id plucked
from the eye of the sun,
Body lifeless, soul writhing
in blasphemous conflict!

Destiny's doormat, acquiescently
condoning the outrage.
Too weak to fight, the body
and soul merely exist.
God! What a price to pay
for gullible ignorance!
The tragedy: All is agony
in the epithet of love.

The Judgment

Grief! Alas! I have grieved over banishment.
I have bravely borne the blow of betrayal;
Felt the agony of supreme humiliation;
And accepted the resultant mockery.

I sought the blessed truth—I found it not.
Colorful lies poured out of dragon mouths,
Flaming with fire and burnt black with deceit,
Emitting words that further shank my courage.

In isolation I have succumbed to fear.
In solitude I am forced to meditate.
The quiet day offers nothing but sadness,
Only an interlude before a new day's toil.

Do you sit judging me in silent stern reproach?
Whilst I with my righteousness deny you?
Because, friend, you sentence me without a word,
And I will not pay forever for my venial sin!

Smile and Remember...

*Again the parting—again the loneliness
envelopes me.*

*Until we meet again, my love,
fare thee well.*

*God protect and embrace you
in His arms*

*Until my soul can rejoice
in your presence*

*And my love can reflect in the
mirror of your eyes.*

*What beauty lies in the ache of
longing!*

*It can only mean deepest affection
And yet...*

*The tragedy of separation is that
there is never enough time.*

*I, the glutton, am never satiated
Nor is my thirst ever quenched.*

*For the wonder of you always starves me
And the hunger never stops.*

*But for now, I'll just
Smile and Remember...*

The Trail Not Chosen

Unsettled, unsure, uncomfortable.
When uncertainties take over
and there is no foreseeable solution,
It's the trail not chosen.
It ends in infinity, ho hum—
depression and delirium.
It's what makes one feel like
skin is crawling or jumping out!
Aye, it is what can not be
soothed at the moment.

No security blanket can help,
certainly no thumb sucking!
No one's shoulder to cry on—
there really is nothing wrong!
Calling a friend doesn't help,
or trying to put on happy airs.
It's just the empty feeling
that all is not right
in the world and its dissipation
probably comes on the morrow.

The Web

Starved, the temptress I seek thee out,
And one by one I take my pick.
Mind and body I absorb thee,
Like a Black Widow to cast thee dead.

The scars of one who hurt me deep
Have mortared stones around my heart.
Begone—I will give you no more, for
Hunger bothers not sleeping bears!

The Wooden Box

The bed is my coffin at night.
The cool sheets my silken shroud,
And the thick blankets, the ground
That covers my livid remains.
I turn in each night with eerie visions
That I might not wake up,
For all is blue and lifeless
In the sea of my imagined death.
I hug the edge of sanity
As I lay in my wooden box—
A quilted carton that cradles my bones
All eaten and plucked clean,
As he took all of me, and left just
Noisy trinkets that rattle in fear...

You're Gone

And the wind plays the harp
As it bends the trees to howling tunes,
Blowing, swishing, shuddering
Everything but the steadfast.

So too the wind song in my heart.
Churning, crushing, straightening
All the fibers—clutching my soul
With searing hurt.

The gale compounds the wounds,
Old and new 'til dying seems
More desirable than life,
And the enemy bludgeons on again.

Healing

Acceptance

To listen—without judgment.
To hear—without malice.
Frightened, who thee understands?

To love—without question.
To know—with acceptance.
Beholden and naked—the flaws.

To see—all the etchings.
To feel—all the trembling.
What star is more brilliant than man?

To cry—somewhere deep from within,
To laugh—like the cuckoo.
Incredible, it is being human.

Ambiguity

Pretending, incognito—
Hiding from reality.
Searching for truth,
Façade of calm.
Feigning what's inside—
No one can guess
The real disguise
Of ambiguity.

Forget and Live

What shall today bring for thee Desiree?
Thy emotions are stripped and bare,
Futilely spent for the world to see.
Your pain and anguish lift their ugly heads,
And vehemence is in your step
As you walk the angry mile.
Today is the continuance of a golden past,
Which is only a memory tomorrow.

Alas! Napoleon's illusion is unearthed—
A fleeting fantasy of thy dreams.
The new day won't let you see him,
Enveloped in a blinding light called "forget."
Perchance tomorrow the hurt will heal,
And optimism will be today's "hello."
Savor no grief, then, for time is passing,
And is only connected by living itself.

Forgiveness

You forgave my insolent frailty
    and my tardiness homeward.
Perfection you sought not,
    only reconciliation.
You waited with regal patience
    for my weighty decision,
Oh, to choose, to choose—
    slow coming—I wept inside.
I cried into my soul ever,
    but found no saving grace.

'Til one day suppressed tears flowed
    from eyes errantly parched blind.
And broken, the dam of denial
    flowed to a new dimension.
And the spirit's breath blew free
    between the kindreds in us.
Dying to self, I came alive once more.
    from a pool of boundless wailing,
To the fountain of wondrous living
    and endless it reached the sea.

Published in the 2005 International Library
of Poetry Anthology
The International Who's Who in Poetry

Look Up!

Look up and out the window of your life
at grey tear drops falling from the maze.
At seasons of joy and sorrow in retrospect,
and love, question or answer, unasked.

Aura unknown, what is the ultimate fate?
Earmarked for strife or docility,
yearning fingers feel rugged scales of desire,
but hide in clapping for misfortune.

Yea, the welts of denial and disappointment,
stalactites of conflict drip in endless pools
searching for the missing counterpart
in the catacombs of mocking memories.

What comfort is the tunic of time?
Put on the dawn of forgetfulness and
feel the silken sheath cover the scorn,
mellowing passions and swallowing hate.

On Lost Love

What pill is there for a heart
shriveled and cold?

Is there a cure for madness
or rebellion brought on by
incessant waiting?

What spectacular transplant,
or feat of surgery can
bring back lost love?

Crypts are filled with
the shrouds of
once hope-filled dreamers.

Strange, there is no sadness,
only melancholia...

The tide ran its course...
It ebbed
and came back renewed.

Picking up the Pieces

From what I had, what have I now?
Attired, I am naked still.
Humbly stripped of the finest lace
I am robbed of pride and heart.

Doubting all, mistrust and hurt,
I bear it smiling all the while.
What thief had stealth to cut me through?
But what of love? Ah, what of it?

Truth! Belief or betray, which road?
Determined, I walk one more mile.
A face—false courage shrieks at me,
And wisdom says, "Pick up the Pieces."

Life's bridges, one to another,
pathways made to forget the past.
I see green meadows up a ways,
But barren when I claim my stake.

What have I seen to wish for more?
Searching for the unknown prize—
Will it glare upon my gaze,
or will I die before I find thee?

Reflections on Today

Today descends like the onset of labor.
It comes invading like smoke.
A tyranny of excuses makes decisions.
Beware of the evil—not known when it comes.

Who bears the evil? My friend or my foe?
What is the evil? Was it once virtue?
The fire's ablaze whilst I cry in my brain.
Errs insignificant compared to life profound.

What is the real issue of life today?
Is it possessing love or is it possessing
love of all other? Perhaps the two are one?
Ah, crying tempts—but answers never come.

And the silence is reigning—ever and ever.
Flicker firelight—the heart knows no other.
The birds sing glory songs—they know no other.
'Tis man who injures, who stumbles, who falls.

This is the creature who causes his ills.
Pains are derived from his living—his needs.
See! It is man, woman, child who journeys ever.
But, behold! Humanity brings each today!

Vespers of a Summer Night

High overhead the moon shines
into the window over my bed.
I sleep.

And the heat of the summer's night
is damp and the breeze blows cool.
I feel.

Still but for nocturnal life
Leaves fall and ripple placid pools.
I dream.

The moon climbs higher, brighter, and
the wind tastes sweetness in the pines.
I know.

Croaking frogs chant lullabies
seducing crickets to their tables.
I breathe.

The sounds of echoes in chase
pass by the sill of my chamber safe.
At peace.

Walking the Edge

The unknown terror—I dread,
follows me night and day,
in time to the rising and setting
of the splendiferous sun.

A dream filled with alarm
wakes me to this subconscious low,
a realm of torture and anxiety,
and I ponder it ever with awe.

Alas! Weeks have not prepared me
for the ultimate, oppressive
events which trigger this dismal,
unquestionable illusion of fright.

Now the real cause is known;
circumstances are at eventide,
and life's work threatens to close
with too many decisions to make.

Behold! The monster is the night.
And, lo, I believe indecision is
the enemy who robs my peace,
and, pray, slay the beast I must!

Woman in Blue

Woman in blue, peer out the rickety door.
    See the light of midday diminished by rain.
Another moment in love's history passed thee by,
    now captured in another man's dream.

Wonderment—what thoughts have you staring out,
    that desolate aperture in an empty house?
Edifice so worn and bleak, fortress cracked and grey.
    lonely and sad like the day? Or reflecting peace?

There—an iridescent pearl clothed in misty blue,
    enfolded in gloom like the arms of a willow.
What sinister songs do you harbor inside the gate,
    sheltered in this structure weatherworn and old?

Memories that flooded each crevice of this abode
    invited fantasies untold—the romance of youth.
Strange, tomorrow your dress may be mellow yellow,
    when sunshine laces your shadow in the door.

Workday Dreams Diminished

How far away are dreams, how far!
The "get ahead" world is ablaze with hope,
while I put away the anvil and mallet,
with grueling weight of the workday done.

Inspired youth and all their flurry,
depart with haste when the fire's doused,
their visions of grandeur are fleeting at best,
as unsought mere reality comes with age.

Truth grips the days with steadfast vice,
and soothes the nights with menthol rub.
Determination fades to get there first—
I will walk, young friend, while you fly.

A Year's Diary of Soliloquies

Jan 13 Life is a river of tears all because I loved too much.
Surely my body is a tomb, a shroud, to mark the
grave of a demised heart.

Jan 15 The silence and snow are overwhelming.
Numb and devoid of emotion, I sit in eerie silence
not hearing your voice. I feel utterly despondent
and helpless. Even Brownie, the mourning dove,
my little emissary has flown from me.

Jan 18 Winter was my favorite season—the snow made
God's presence so near. Now all I feel is the cold
and think of another's desire for spring—ah,
to be reborn again.

Jan 20 The trees are covered in crystal sheaths
like halos. I put on my shroud of misery again.

Jan 21 An unexpected warm rain has melted the snow
betraying a brown, barren, muddy earth. Another
grim day.

Jan 28 A baby...fragile and yet it has the supreme
strength of being—the weakness and yet the
mighty power to command hearts!

Jan 31 Time will either become my friend or my
enemy for with its passing I shall succumb to its
desires or endure its breaking into a million pieces.

Feb. 1   Sweet sorrow is so intent—to sob with desire
and possess a burning ache. My little dove is covered
with snow. My heart wants to bring him in from the
cold to dry his wet feathers and warm his small existence.
It is quiet. I hear my heart beating and my thoughts
reverberate the words "I love you."

Feb 2   How shallow are well-meaning friends' thoughts and
ramblings. I sit in complete dismay at what once made me
cordially laugh. Their feeble minds command mouths to
speak ambiguous and unintelligible words which are
irrevocably spent on my unlistening ears.

Feb 7   In the creeping shadows that are the last hint
of night, I hear a familiar voice saying, "Good morning,
Love." I awake to clouds sprinkling more confetti upon us.

Feb 13   I am the wedge that splits and yet I can never
claim the pieces.

Feb 22   I am the last crumbling, shaking leaf on a tree
of a spent autumn, waiting for the final gale to sever
me from its branch forever!

Feb 26   The restless troublesome night has turned into
a placid and memorable dawn. The sweetness of life
is within me, and I revel in its mystery.

Mar 9   Philosophy? We start life as happy children, grow into
uncertain adults, and wait for death in old age. Life!

Mar 30   Real death seems to come in loving and not having.
Real pain is in wanting and not realizing the evasive
dream.

Apr 19   I feel like a tissue that has gone through the laundry
and came out in clumps of bits and pieces. It's so
pathetic I could laugh hysterically, except for one
thing—it isn't funny!

Jun 12   As I gaze in the mirror, I see the sheen of chestnut brown hair and I think how my loved one probably looked down upon me with pleasure—for I know he found me beautiful.

Jun 22   The balloon is squeezing itself to death with each little escape of air. How true!!!

Jun 27   It's funny how the words flow on paper when one is depressed, but happiness is something to share with another in person!

Jul 8   Wisdom? Perhaps wisdom comes when one realizes not everything is known. The summation of one's life then is to find out how ignorant we are after all!

Jul 14   Again I hide inside myself. I am flying high— I want to forget I need you but I am a neon sign reflecting my endless thoughts like banners of crepe paper.

Jul 29   You hypocrite!!! Bones entombed by the white granite sepulcher. Dwell on the sacrilege of living, fool! It is all a joke, you know! Hoping against hope for a change of heart! Damn it!!

Aug 3   In two hours-time I have experienced all range of emotions imaginable. I awoke nervous, indifferent, then crying and desperate, then angry and now calm and drained. I am indeed dumb!

Aug 10   Today the Queen's Lace juts to the sky in solemn dignity while the blue wildflowers covering the courtyards of the meadow bend their heads in quiet submittance.

Aug 11   Duped and dumped! The joke is always on the king's fool! Clown, dry thy smeared eyes and wash the stains from thy garment. Put on a feeling of acquiescence called, "plodding along."

Aug 14 I look into the window of God and see
fall is in the air. Dew is on the grass in the morning
and the wind has changed its flavor. Scent: early winter.
Ah, but my heart is already full of ice anyway...

Sep 3 My fate has been handed down like the sentence of
the guillotine. It is terrifying that events in one's life
cannot be controlled. I feel like the hub of a spoked
wheel and don't know which spoke I rely on the most.

Sep 12 The pounding in my brain increases in volume
only to make me deaf and dumb to my intelligence.
In the end my heart lies panting on the floor when I
remember. Now to put my life all back together again,
wrapping all in a package of patience!

Sep 21 I miss thee most in the quiet hours, but even
in a crowd, I walk alone...

Oct 12 The past is like looking through a field thick with
misty fog. Lately each day seems to be the same—
nondescript—busy. A day is a day—and God knows,
a night is a lonely night.

Oct 14 Two ships passing in the night...lonely, quiet motion
like the lurching, dark, inky waters on a moonless night.

Oct 15 God, I love you...you know what's in my heart. Can I
be so bad that on Judgment Day You would deny me??

Oct 17 I want to hear music in my life but the serenades
have ceased to exist. Only a vanishing phantom do
I crave—but the light is getting dimmer...

Oct 19 The lamp is out! No more is the lighthouse standing
in the darkness guiding my ship to port. A strong wind
swept over the flame and choked it 'til it flickered and died.
Now in the blackness, a ghost ship wanders the inky waters
aimlessly groping for love. The lonely blast of its piercing
alert sounds for miles around searching for the other vessel
to "pass in the night." It comes not...

Oct 24   Strange, one can look at certain situations and
         already foresee the inevitable. The sinister bearer
         of confusion and doubt stays as close as a shadow
         paces its master in the sun.

Oct 25   I'm in a room filled with people laughing, joking,
         pandemonium. I don't belong—I should escape and
         run to the "thing" I am missing in my life. There is grass—
         the smell of it like burning flesh—maybe it's hellfire. A den
         of inequity, people drunk with denial of all that is moral
         and good. I flee for my life!

Oct 26   Infinitum—forever—I am. Beyond the human mind's
         capacity to understand, that is what I believe my being is.

Oct 28   A new philosophy for me—love not, lest ye be hurt. Giving
         oneself never seems to reap the best harvest. Leave open a
         flank and the enemy will destroy you. I am exiled from
         myself—there is no inner peace...

Nov 10   A gloomy day outside—'tis gloomier though to face
         each other all day long with empty hearts and contempt
         in our brains—quiet, but for the storms building inside...

Nov 13   Today I am the snowbird—I lift my wings as the
         snowflakes melt on my uplifted face. I am again born in
         winter. This is my beginning...these are my roots.

Dec 13   Strange bird that I am—out of chaos, I find confidence.

Dec 27   Virtue screams at me everywhere, but treason lurks
         in the amphitheatre of my life probing and prickling at my
         already tattered existence. I am a fool...

Dec 31   Man is clutter; man is doing; man is never done.
         And so life goes on. On this last day of the year I am
         still the same person I was before—maybe smarter,
         maybe not. But I've endured. I've lived. As I close this
         year's diary, I turn the page to a new chapter in my life—
         turning from pages that can never be rewritten or redone.
         I relinquish my rights to the past tonight and tomorrow
         I will step, renewed, into the future.

* * * * * * *

A New Life and Love

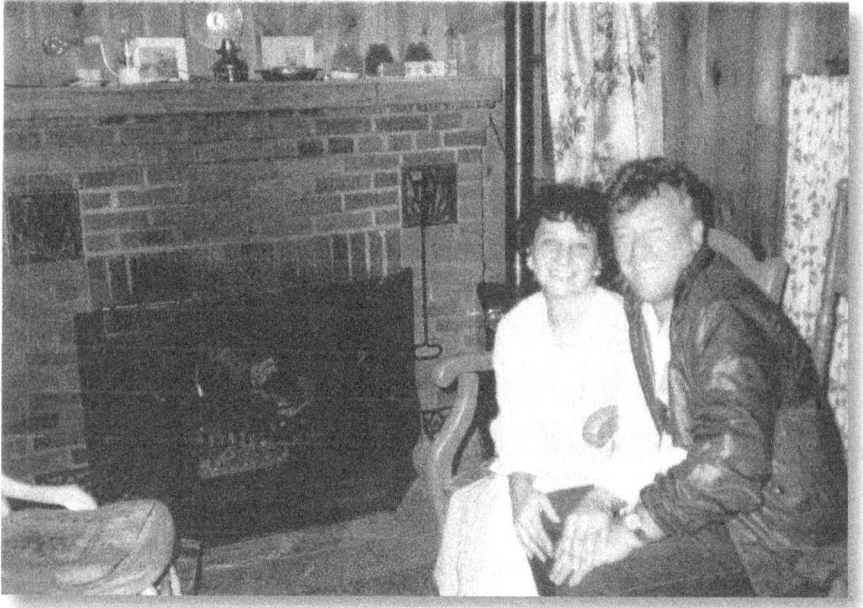

The Afterglow

The fire glows with the memories of
hours past.
Molten embers like the sunrise simmer
in loving thoughts.
Dreams are the flames that lick and
taste the wood;
The logs rest, one against the other,
like lovers snuggled.
Consumed, their love burns bright
But does not disintegrate.
Exploding sparks descend into the ash,
Like fireworks dazzle a leadened sky.
Moments are warm coals--orange, alive
And time is not.

A Date with a Divine Accident

In a forest glade that harbors truth,
    The wind compels the pines to sing.
Benevolent Love, my Divine Accident,
    What secret meets the earth and sky?

Peace descends on meadows yawning,
    Enticing soles to tread the stillness.
Lovers feel the magic splendor,
    Knowing dreams for moments exist.

Hear the sighs of drooping flowers,
    Orange, yellow and purple gems.
Prayerful chums to pearls of dew,
    That lace the velvet green cascade.

Destiny, Love, divinely accidental,
    Like golden joy in rustling leaves.
Or shimmering wishes in water pools.
    Oh, sun of precious earth, lift my heart!

Published in the 2005 International Library of
Poetry anthology
A Surrender to the Moon

The Endorphins Are Comin'

Ah! There's a pain in my neck!
Oh, just what I need at dinnertime!
When lo and behold, my son, Carel, is here
Asking if he can help.

"I'll rub your neck, Mom,"
Says he with a beguiling smile.
"Okay," says I, while peeling
The potatoes ever slowly to a halt.

"Oh, that feels good, son--
You could put me to sleep."
I stop peeling and the endorphins
Take over and keep on comin'.

Hear me sigh as I'm in a meltdown---
How his gentle hands upon my
Aching neck and shoulders
Obey his commands to relax!

Now I think to myself—
How good it is to be a Mom
When blessings and love like this
Waltz in unannounced!

The Homecoming

The beauty of my life is filled with
the homecoming of your smile.
Sorrows prevailing simply vanish
in the glint of your eyes.
A love I've never known comes alive
in a kiss of acceptance.
I am spellbound in a tender embrace
that carries me to heaven.

How beholdingly wondrous it is
to have such trust and security!
Does destiny hold the "8th Wonder
of the World" in my realm?
In a haven of piety I find peace
in the spirit of thy favored soul,
And in your song and laughter the
stairway to God's gate of happiness.

continued

With patience and humility I'm inspired
to seek charity and compassion.
I've found reward in giving,
and love is the ultimate prize.
In your tenderness I've found comfort
in a torrid ocean of troubles.
And life's beauty lingers every day
that I have been your cherished bride.

My love, I walked the forest glade
and found a flower—a
flower God had planted just for me.
I picked it by Divine Accident
and found in all of creation,
There is no one—no one like you...

On Love...

Run fast, run wild soaring spirit!
Heart take flight like the mourning dove!
Be free and aspire to the epitome of virtues!
Love—it is the yoke of a happy heart!

The Real Poet's Laurel

You are the poet!
I write, but you fathom.
I compose,
But you understand.
For this,
You wear the laurel.
You are the greater,
And I the least!

Sons of Life's Longing

See their young handsome faces,
Sun-browned and finely chiseled,
As they turn toward the door.

They walk with a man's easy gait,
All masculine and powerful,
Hungry for more than tacos,

And hoping for the extreme adventure.
Life is cool wonder—
Every moment a new beginning.

Three futures determined
Only by their dreams.
With assured confidence,

The day is theirs to explore.
Calmly they embrace life's
Longing for itself.

Published in the 2006 International Library of Poetry anthology
The Best Poems and Poets of 2005

Timeless

I look at your picture, the one I tucked away.
So many memories—
each day filled to capacity.
No place to hide from the yearning.
The world begins and ends with you, little bird.
And the sun shines through
clouds that mar the way.

I daydream of slumber—spending
quiet nights in gentle, waiting arms.
Longing to wake to smiling
eyes that hold me captive—
conquest of desire and hours of chatter.
Seeking comfort in tearful revelations
finding strength in endless optimism.

No one can describe the happiness
of tender, intimate love.
There the silence is filled
with caring and time stands still.
Your breath is mine as we kiss.
My soul soars to heavenly
heights in your rhapsody.

Neither of us exists—we
are now one person.
There is no turning back,
For when love is given,
It comes back twice—it is never lost!
Time is but the fortress
that cements love forever.
But only God can bless it.

Events Along The Way

The Carcinoma

In Memory of Rena Peggie, 12-21-98_

What is the fear that torments man,
clutching like the trellis vine?
It finds a hole in places where
healers' hands cannot impose.
It drags its feet through blood and bone.
It slithers through each waking thought.
Immortal not, we dread the day
when the "cord" of life is cut.

Destroy the evil that curses "well,"
invading as it does one's health.
Burn the choking, fibrous fingers,
enveloping all that's good and new.
Shed the winding, curious climb,
sprawling through the infinite maze,
crying, "My God, my God, why me?"
thinking what future dream I will not see.

See hideous quirks on life are played,
pray, death is welcome to the pain.
In sleep, life is again simply sweet,
as wretched bodies stave relief from reality.
Is this a macabre tribute to death?
Or rather empathy for those who live?
Frantically, each waits for the first sign
that will crush hearts like a vice.

continued

Ah, mankind, we equally share the pain...
Unasked for birth—unwanted death.
And in between, living, loving and learning.
Escape: never; succumb: always! Futility!
But oh, the common chains of human bondage,
linking one another, inception to ultimatum,
cemented forever in knowledge acquired.
Inseparable, triumphant, we are the living end!

Dad, Mover of Cars

Six vehicles parked in our drive,
One for each human plus one,
That one pulls the trailer—
Maybe twice a year!

Now listen to my story,
It's funny but it's true,
In all seasons, each and every day
Dad moves or cleans the cars anew.

You see, if not done the night before,
The cars need be arranged,
For all residents in our house
Their varied schedules made.

So Dad, first one up, each morning
Attends cars like a junk yard dog,
This one needs out at 7 a.m.--
This one is at eight!

Shifting, parking, moving along,
Out come our hurried sons,
Donut and coffee in hand,
Saying, "Thanks, Dad!"

The Empty Stage

A Play's Finale

Splintered and scratched, wooden stage so bare,
Actors have gone and audience glare.
Sweltering lights have dimmed to dark,
Quiet sound where applause was stark.

Warped, creaking boards of set and frame,
Playing medleys new minstrels claim.
Voiceless sounds o'er microphones,
Shapeless costumes weep where thrown.

An eerie guard velvet curtains keep,
Watching the lifeless properties sleep.
'Til 'company' gives men's words a soul,
And damsels dance to a well-worn scroll.

From Age To Old Age

Oh doubtful times! Behold being confused, and afraid.
Alone, lost and uncertain—health is frail.
Visitors are few—knowledge escaping and memory wanes.
Friends are long gone and decisions too many.
Changes are overwhelming—common sense, elusive.
Overtaken with worry, and death looms at the door.

Days of endless waiting—imagining, anticipating.
Silence and then moments of agitation.
Years fly by and age fades like yellowed newspaper.
The fate foreseen at 50—the sum of parents and more!
We mirror the portraits of old timers on the wall,
Familiar and how surprisingly the same!

Craving relief from aches and pains—in reality, sorrows;
Seeking comfort from children once comforted.
And feigning apologies for being blind and lame.
Never forgetting, even though thoughts are dimmer,
the integrity and the rambling paths of youth, and the
independence and love known and once treasured.

Oddly, we peer in the mirror to see our soul's reflection,
the only face that one has known—it is timeless.
The face of genes since our time began—from age to old age.

Lady, Did You Know

(In Memory of Wilhelmina & Theodore Mineur)

Lady, did you know
that you would bear
such good sons and daughters?

Caring for you and Dad—
caring for each other,
year after precious year.

Had you ever thought
how fine and upstanding
each would become one day?

Now that you're in heaven
along with loving Dad,
they still celebrate your lives.

Anniversaries, birthdays,
events from long ago.
Tearful stories all remembered.

Fondly, your children
even though far apart,
stay together in kindred spirit.

For the day when they will see
their Mom and Dad again
Lady, did you know
how much they loved you!

Judgment: Prison—Penalty—Time!

Here we are, sitting in the lobby of the county jail.
Destination: See our kin—incarcerated for misdemeanors.
We are meek and humbled and await the visit like everyone there.
Sparsely furnished with plastic, molded, unmatched chairs.
Eclectic textures and uncoordinated colors on floors and walls.
Brown lockers, 25 cents. TV monitor cameras, low voices
speaking quietly, embarrassed, telling stories of each scenario.
People—old and young, black and white and all in between,
poorly or richly attired—all waiting for the loud speaker...
"Attention: 1:30 p.m. registered visitors line up."
Filing through the "detector," coatless and bagless, arms empty save
the nervous twisting and wrying of hands,
we pause at the steel door—the portal of the imprisoned—we wait.
The grinding sound of the first door thudding open.
The second door, prison's gate, thudding shut! Locked in!
The elevator takes the visitors to the upper floors,
each privately in their own thoughts—not a sound is made.
We exit on the floor where the prisoners wait—
lover, mother, wife, sister, brother, father, or friend.
Phones to the inmates are picked up simultaneously.
Visits begin—the initial fumbling of greetings and a week's
worth of news to tell—in 25 minutes, the time allotted!
Sadness is lifted—only for the moment. Lots to tell and say.

continued

The condition is one of enduring—of waiting.
Time goes slowly for those who pay for their crimes.
For those who wait outside, agony is evident in tears.
Kids don't know why Dad's not home—Mom reacquaints
them—again.
All inmates are not "evil" but a compilation of many fragments--
perhaps those of neglect, abuse or indifference.
And so, the speaker announces time is up. Watching those leaving,
an array of humans with diverse cultures, customs, feelings, ideas.
Different upbringings, not to the standards of many—
some not taught or loved or disciplined at all.
Presently, they are on a journey—only God knows where.
All equal in an equal environment with equal dress and
equal "billing," serving time for a myriad of offenses.
Judgment: Prison. Penalty: Time!

Salt & Pepper

(For Patrick and Ann)

Salt and pepper—the spices of life...
they make the most of each gourmet creation,
adding flavor, color, texture, and taste.
They bring out the best in everything
and they add zest to ho-hum cuisine.
By using them with discretion
you will confidently create and experiment.

Moderation is prudently suggested—
not too much—not too little—just enough!

Like everything in life, spice
makes it interesting; spice makes it fun.
So, Patrick and Ann, in your wedded life
be the salt and pepper—make every day
spicy and make every day fun!
With the right ingredients, with God,
with thoughts of family, a little luck, and of course,
Salt and Pepper, you'll savor the love.

Toby

Abby

Misty

Chloe

Smokey

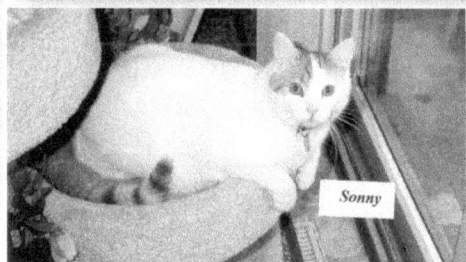
Sonny

Six Cats in My Care

Where are you, buddies of mine?
One half dozen smiling meows,
curled up, sleeping on the couch,
lying sprawled out on my bed.

Perched high up on cabinets
or lounged 'neath the dining table.
I see you not 'til stomachs growl,
and interests piqued by smell or sound.

Sometimes yearning for a pat,
or scratching underneath a chin.
Tumbling after one another,
chasing tails or playing "king,"

Loving looks, mews in chorus
stretched out paws that stop me still.
Nips to let me know that you're there.
It's time to pet with gentle touch.

And most of all, let you know you're loved.

Sleeping Giants

Wishes--how we long for them to come true.
We pray, we pine, we plan, we fantasize.
Alas, when will they materialize??

Then, one by one the sleeping giants awake,
Behold each one yawns, growls and jolts us
Making our lives more intolerable than before.

"Be careful what you wish..." in my brain I hear
Wary now, I retreat into my silent world
And wish I had not stirred the brew.

A time will come when I will regress again,
Into a place where it all began...
The liquid amber of my being--the womb.

Then will I be free of this eternal search,
The quest and allure of evasive happiness,
For then will I be upon the lap of God.

Spiritual Reflections

A Beautiful Soul

I am the love I see in the eyes
of a soul too beautiful to claim.
In this mirror, a reflection
of God is revealed.
It is my true love,
And I am one in prayer with thee.

The Call

Mary, I have not forgotten you.
Now and then I call and
tenderly gain your attention;
your thoughts are so far away.

I remember your youth,
so fervently did you attend me.
Sometimes I think now you're
busily occupied with trivia.

That is when I whisper
and call your name—my name.
"Come, come my dear child.
It is my special day."

Come celebrate with me my birth
and visit my Son—the 8th of September.
Honor me with your love and faith
for my name's sake on the 12th as well.

Twice I have done just that,
and twice you have responded.
I murmured softly in your ear,
and met you at the altar of my Love.

continued

There you were as if
frozen in time—the same.
I know you now, my little one,
fervent and pious ever aged.

The peace I bring you,
makes me glad to be your mother.
I see your struggles,
I hear your pleas as I do for all men.

I am your Mother—your friend
and I know all that is.
Have faith in me always
and in time you will be mine.

I have not forgotten you
dearest namesake, Mary.
Please don't forget me and that
I'll always love you.

Christmas Love

Little child so small and slight, in that manger lay,
Order all things to thy hands in such a loving way.
Reach inside my heart this night and fill an empty soul,
Warm me with thy cherub smile, my life is icy cold.

Little Lord, I've lost my way, the road is dark and damp,
I need thee Star of Bethlehem, to be my guiding lamp.
Oh, sweet Jesus, Holy Babe! Tiny Child Devine!
My only prayer this night is love—God of Love, be mine.

The King and I

What awe bespeaks this noble heart
while death becomes her constant friend.
What vast abyss separates life from death—
Is it but a beam of radiant light?
Eminent friend, you traitor too,
How can thy stealth smite my breath,
and transubstantiate this flesh
into the dust from whence it came.

O terrible fear that grips my heart
with fingers clutched like vines.
Art thou more afeard of the sickness
then of the end itself?
Woe besets ignorant ears, unhearing ears,
as frightened tongues speak through my pen.
O wretched body decaying so,
why must I know death to know life?

Creature of mud, you bend your frame
and time hurries on the days.
Evil draws awful crow's feet
decaying tissue and bone.
But when that dreadful moment comes,
when all the world stands still,
into what harbor will I drift aground,
or port unknown dwell forever?

continued

Will subterranean fires singe my feet,
Where ghastly bodies cry and burn,
screaming, wailing, uncontrolled
madness, everything unconsumed.
Or look safely to cool waters in Galilee
where God's Trinity I see.
Discarding body of bone for light,
and dying into eternal life.

Shedding skins of mother earth,
I bathe in grace sublime.
Garments of illumination I put on
for the wedding feast of King and I.

Mary Minjeur

Home of All Homes

In death's wake I will be triumphant!
Pain dissolves like snow in spring.
And the Son is now my only realm,
for I have found a better place.
Untouched, unspoiled by Satan's tinge,
and finally seeing through blinded eyes
I view the awesome face of Him—

Deity I feared before I knew
what love His countenance emanates.
In a hundred years of earthly strife,
I'll never know more tranquil life—
A home of homes to rest always
of timeless joy and endless days,
forever in the heart of God.

Published in the 2008 winter anthology
By Noble House, Centres of Expression

The Intelligent Designer

I am the tree of unequaled strength.
　　I stand guard over earthly things.
I attest to decades of life and death,
　　And see joy and sorrow incarnate.

I am the stone that stubs a toe.
　　I am cursed and thrown but do not break.
I fall, I roll, I skim, I lay.
　　Laden and heavy, the earth is me.

I am the sky— the cerulean blue.
　　I am endless space—infinity of black.
I cradle the world with day and night,
　　And hold the universe steadfast.

I am the sun, I am the moon, and
　　I am the stars that give men light.
I am the center, the scorching fire.
　　Master, I reside in every heart.

I am the babe, I am the miracle.
　　I am forever incomprehensible.
I am timeless wisdom, I am Love always.
　　I am the Intelligent Designer.

Published in the 2006 Noble House anthology,
Songs of Honour

The Last Day

Tenaciously I await the last day.
The hours prior to a dream fulfilled.
Will it be love's return, old or new,
or a time when mothers meet their sons.

Love's fulfillment after long absence,
or the smell of familiar places long denied.
Returning from a cold and lonely place,
whether it be war, work or play.

Tender is the thought of home—of home...
Chamber of memories held fast by time,
stretching contentment like a sleeping cat,
and placid routine like birds at the feeder.

Hour by hour the minutes go past,
and then—and then—I am there!
I am there—I am really there—the last day.
Trembling I kiss the threshold of tomorrow.

Mourning Song

Mourning song, the faint drum roll,
heard softly in the hush.
Quiet time for life's last glimpse
Aye, before the Judgment bares.

All is done; the seeds are sown,
never more to taste life sweet.
Thy fruits, rich or barren be,
mirrored now for thee to see.

Man, what thoughts had you alive,
think of knowledge put to rest.
Dreams and feelings made you be,
loving almost made you whole.

Now the Chariot of God is near,
racing for thy soul.
Beat winged hoofs in torrid flames,
snatch thee from the demon's hold.

See the lyres sweetly play,
while trumpets blare His glory.
Victory o'er death is nigh,
and bells of triumph toll "Justice!"

Swell, oh song, to endless heights!
Angels shout the chorus, tell,
resound thy earthly goodness,
and joyful to thy God, oh sing!!

The Sacred Promise

Tears of blood fall from swollen eyes.
Drop by drop they shimmer to the ground.
A wounded heart is shattered through,
And Love has paid Man's debt forever.

Soaring With the Lord

Lord, my heart wants to soar with you!!!
How great is thy love and thy spirit!
Alas, I am not ready by your own words,
suffering—I need to do "more time."

Oh, but the agony of waiting and being left behind!
How much grief does one encompass?
How much can the human vessel hold?
Life is full of woe and empty but for you!

Where does my crooked, marred path lead?
Guide me, oh my Savior, guide me!
My life is forever in your gentle hands!
Save me from all needless worry and harm!

Make me ready Lord; make me your soft clay,
Mold and shape me into the pottery you will.
When I am tested by fire, let me rise up shining as gold,
Like the dove whose wings yearn for the sky.

continued

Purify my heart and make me a kinder being.
Erase my evil ways so I will be pure of mind.
Cleanse my thoughts of self-centeredness,
Make me your chalice of flowing generosity.

My God, do not forsake me in my hour of need.
Time and sorrows grow like briars in my path,
Like the jungle, vines grope to strangle me.
Yet the lamp is ahead and I see your light.

I am spent and shaken without your strength;
I am nothing yet you have made me your child.
I am unworthy and insignificant, and I am so desperate.
Claim me Lord, for I want nothing but you.

Where else can I go to find the compassion you give?
In what manner can peace descend to me
like the soft snow settling on my cheeks in winter?
You have eternal life and you are my happiness!

The branches of the trees lift their arms to you,
and I too reach for your comfort and protection.
There my soul is secure and content like a sleeping babe.
Abba, I breathe easy laughing in your embrace.

Oh, turn not away from me in displeasure or disgust!
Forgive me my stupidity and my transgressions.
Listen to my pleas; they are the creature's way—my way—
My feeble way of saying, Father, Creator, I love you.

Haiku Harvest and Reflections In Poetry

A Haiku Harvest

Pristine, clear, scented—
dew kisses the rose petal,
fragile, soft beauty!

Catacombs of light
spewing alabaster glare
on ancient footsteps.

Frozen in time warp,
winter cactus in full bloom,
nondescript and pale.

Shades of blue skylight,
cerulean reflections,
water to disturb.

Another fine day,
folds into the night once more,
renewing God's love.

Dawn of creation,
daily gift since time began,
love is beholden.

Magnificent morn!
Bridal veil of snowy white,
spills to mossy glen.

Dewey, misty, morn.
Present in the majesty
of dawn's early light.

Northern Lights ablaze,
flare 'cross the indigo blue,
spellbind those who stare.

A mid-summer's day,
wrought in lacy radiance,
invite soles to tread.

Flames of jagged gold,
permeate asphalt night skies,
white waves swell with tides.

The sea is calling,
beckoning since time began
life in infancy.

The sword's edge of night,
laden with turbulent tears,
and grey at its end.

Billowing flower,
with scarlet eye beholding--
beckons to Ms. Bee.

Burnt sienna sky,
hovering over the plains,
evidence the night.

Water flowing e'er,
trailing through the centuries,
always toward the sea.

Beams of sunlight,
radiant, warming, aglow,
pervade dense woodlands.

Placid lake mirrors
stormy peaks of misty white,
making themselves known.

Streaks of red embers
permeate approaching night,
signaling day's end.

Gnarled fingers pointing
toward the setting sun's embrace
foreboding day's end.

The blackness of night
takes over where daylight ends—
in oblivion.

Monstrous mushroom cloud,
yawning o'er the blue vista,
churning toward the sea.

Stillness of morning,
the chill of dew still clinging,
bird songs bring the day.

Beauteous tendrils,
with crimson trumpets in place,
envelope fenceposts.

Sword of sunlight's shaft,
piercing the murky lagoon
teeming with new life.

The bumps, twists, and turns,
reflect the paths be trodden
on life's rocky roads.

Earth at peace slumbers,
awaiting newness of dawn,
hues of life's longing.

Prelude to winter,
snow-covered peaks grow daily;
summer ebbs away.

I hear Joshua
calling in the distance,
rise shepherd—follow.

Peace descends on earth,
tumultuous worlds fighting,
give way to the night.

Waves of fallen leaves,
crunches under every step,
grinds to earth once more.

Stepping stones across
the resplendent babbling brook,
paths to the unknown.

Rushing water flows,
pooling in the riverbeds,
grumbling toward the sea.

Splashes of crimson,
lace the aperture in frames
of fall's brilliance.

What fragile array,
hidden in grotesque shadows,
blooms in the darkness.

Archaic wonder
colossal ribbon of blue!
From stone age to aged.

Moonbeam of color,
geranium soft and pink,
nestled in green shams.

Luminous light beam!
Cathedral in dense forest—
does God peer inside?

Sublime universe,
visible to everyone
who has eyes to see!

See the petals yearn,
open—yawning to the sun,
all is well today.

Underground wonders,
caverns and caches, buried still,
hollows left to find.

Labyrinth ensnarled,
frenzied knot of twisted vines,
entraps the tree's life.

A crystal palace,
shades of frozen mist and air,
captures this moment.

Ruby red glory,
pinched lightly by hungry moth,
spreading innocence.

Duped thoughts swirl the mind,
ripples made by a plunked stone,
defining a life.

Mushroom scene delight,
nature toils with little stress,
for us to witness.

Great ball of fire!
Setting west 'til the 'morrow,
rests after day's toil.

Reflections I see,
mirrored in the shining glade,
showcasing the trees.

On the horizon,
ominous storm clouds gather,
stern awakening.

Burnt umber night sky,
background to a feathered palm,
sunset brings us peace.

Thunderous power,
flowing in foamy silver
brine—somewhere, nowhere.

Centuries he guards,
slumbering sloth of the tree,
yawn and stretch your limbs!

Burnt umber night sky,
sunlight sinks to Neptune's grave,
sets 'til the morrow.

Tree gnarled and twisted,
centuries of life unfurled,
defining a life.

White bark of the birch,
like a candle in the dark,
glows in forests green.

View the burning bush,
wild fires spread their havoc,
unconsumed daily.

Grey, grey stormy day.
drags spirits to somber calm,
drifting toward the bog.

Beyond the blizzard,
forest through snowy valleys,
lies the birth of spring.

Dusk—sultry sunset,
nocturnal creatures waiting--
dinner is the plan.

The prism appears,
arching colors 'cross the sky,
as He first promised.

Caverns of blizzards,
snow from so long, long ago.
time in frozen ice.

Significant woe,
stark cumulous clouds threaten
to spoil the sunset.

Reflections in Poetry

- *Glorious beer, drunken night, toasting in dawn's light!*
  Waging war, dreams of fight, braving tooth and byte!

- *And heaven is beyond, the sun, moon, planets and*
  stars, waiting for life's end, desiring reward.

- *The fire tingling red crossed beyond Northern Lights,*
  to stars, sun, and planets rewarding each of us tonight.

- *So ghostly moon reflecting, from fox to wildfowl flight.*
  Moonlight illumines shadows dark, answering ebbing night!

- *Beyond ambitions and reminiscence, turning broken hands,*
  I wandered through memories' fields, and stepped by my youth.

- *Greeks remember a time transcendent, Apollo prominently placed,*
  reached heavenward inspiring amorous tales of spirits and myths.

- *We wouldn't harm anything in life, if we looked beyond our*
  personal desires.

- Grey silhouettes on the shoreline watch stormy wind in swelling oceans, waves crashing, scattering footprints to the tides.

- Beneath the twisted mulberry tree, cracked, hollow, and arched, the opossum found a cozy den.

- On dusty shelves, through stacks of books, and yellowed cards, we rummaged together looking to find loves faded promises.

- Phosphorous caverns in dark subways swiftly winding along the rails, graffiti collage illuminating pillars where commuters huddle in shadows.

- His son's favorite mask, warped, tattered and frail from time, was found outside in spring, touched by scents of earthy pine.

- Love's conscience was divinely tortured by specters illuminant of innocence.

- The stars beyond patiently stay, tingling, like rain that floats in soft breaking clouds.

- Shakespeare's nightmarish Macbeth, stunned and bleeding bloke, overthrown, broken, lunging to his death.

- The gray horizon languidly drifts across silvery, misty waters, encompassing love's soft image mingling with tomorrow.

- Wrinkled, dappled leaves whisper through dancing shadows— relics of time, immortality's thoughts twirling in air soaring 'round a caressing sea.

- Sailing through waters of chance, man-made commands asea, when storm begs calm, a glance to the Creator responds.

- God promised Moses a land where freedom lives,
  no longer slaves to death, but thirsting for love.

- I walked the overgrown thorn bushes finding ruins, where
  moss-covered paths kiss time and memories that strayed.

- Enchanted, youthful lovers sigh, whispering sweet desires,
  from once chimed hours to cobblestoned secrets and silence.

- The easel of drawings in pastel colors and charcoal sketch,
  marred the living gallery of the outstanding sunset.

- Love daily touches life, patiently rewarding
  us in our personal hopes of heaven.

- Oh tragic irrevocable thoughts, horrified memories of hideous
  things, encircle profoundly the hated master of foolery.

- The smiling innocent infant borne into a loving fate of desire.

- Dilapidated and old, the weary couple, beneath the weight
  of antique dreams, escape and fade gently into oblivion.

- Remember honeyed crescent moons and delicious pine
  mist darkness where perfect sultry love was found.

- The collection of artistic poetry resembled a mirror
  reflecting the writer's honorable hopes.

- *Squirrels bury helmeted nuts, hoping to find them in spring.*

- *Carefully and peacefully she stepped, shoulders hunched before lying quietly on the soft divan.*

- *Beyond heaven awaits our hearts desire for God's love.*

- *Autumn's brown chrysalis on a yellowed leaf, turns into a silky butterfly jaunting happily to fleurs-de-lis in spring.*

- *Conquering the impossible, obliterating the passion, annihilating the love, another savage victory!*

- *'Neath the hot crimson sun, solitude in outstretched arms, quiet dimension from haze to compulsive embrace.*

- *The wonderments of the starry heavens overshadows the showcase of the soft white glittering snows.*

- *Hauntingly crystal—it's finger-painting offshoots of breath frozen in time.*

- *Time nor strife changes life's longing to be happy.*

- *Her warm and tempting smile and her desirous soft embrace, ended mawkishly in a stutter!*

- *Tales unequaled linger on o'er the death of a beloved Pope.*

- *Her lemony skin, fragrant and pale, lady against the grey fog, oblivious to yesterday, and journeying to forever.*

- *Between clouds of good and evil is the curse of requited love.*

- *Everything was silently burning in the surrounding sun-swept dawn, like autumn's red painted canvas.*

- *Tragedy embraces pain, portraits of obscurity, and photographs of disaster paints enraged panic.*

- *Blue gravestone unimpeded weeping in the silence, the stillness of death cloaked in the shadows.*

- *Through centuries sublimated, hidden mysteries, subtle and yet strange, reveal the harsh chaos of jealousy.*

- *Quivering shadows wilted in November's blackness, a cruel end casts a burnished throne on a brilliant sunrise!*

- *In life, the wonder of being is a simple soul passing from heaven to earth for a while.*

- *The cat—sleepy eyed and gentle, perched quietly on the verandah in the shade of the golden bougainvillea.*

- *A silvery moon is a giant globe where night's voyage ends.*

- *Savor change—it is the spice of life!*

- *Bundled brown sagebrush, dry gulched from summer's end, bound for winter's burning and prompting fireside warmth.*

- *A thousand unsteady fingers scratch the wall, shuffling to the kitchen in the rest home.*

- *Stately spring Magnolias delight bursts of purple crocuses and yellow daffodils in the dingy brown snow beds.*

- *Battered thieves, three decades lost, now hang from the yardarm.*

- *The mystery of innocence is the divinity of promise.*

- *Nighttime sanctuary, water laps the boat while the music of violins and mandolins lives in my breast.*

- *Splashing turtles barely clutching land, ramble across the ponds, presenting their heads.*

- *Memory surrounds the quiet glory of a young man downtrodden come home.*

- *Sunlight streaking like a silky blanket warming threadbare memories reposing in familiar places.*

- *Performances long-rehearsed, acknowledged and applauded, remain lasting and sentimental memories.*

- *Tiny birds sleeping softly inside white tipped branches, are cozily sheltered from the snow.*

- *Fires of heaven, sun, moon, and stars, beyond time infinity, waiting patiently for peace.*

- *The willow and poplars plead eagerly with the wind to cease its endless gale.*

＊ ＊ ＊ ＊ ＊ ＊ ＊

Remembering Tim

Remembering Tim

Tim was adopted and came to us at the age of eight weeks. Bill and I were thankful and happy to have a child we could nurture and love. He was a beautiful blonde and blue-eyed baby. In time, **Tim grew to be a tall and handsome guy.** He was our only child and we did everything with him, but mostly, we gave him our love and ourselves.

In his youth, he did all the things a normal boy liked to do. He loved sports, swimming, fishing, camping, his dog, and hanging out with neighborhood boys. In high school he enjoyed being a member of the Civil Air Patrol and reading aviation magazines. Although not very academic, he was never any trouble in school. On Sundays he attended church with us, was polite, good natured, and seemed happy. After high school he enlisted for four years in the **United States Marines.**

We were proud of him as he went through basic training, coming home with his form-fitting uniform, shaved head, and trim, hard body. We relished the fact that he was becoming a man and doing something good for his country. **He served in the Gulf War** and we were so grateful when he came home unharmed. We pictured a bright future for him, but he began making bad choices. At the very end of his service, he was generally discharged after a severe altercation with another man over his girlfriend at the time. That was the beginning of his downfall.

His first son was born two days before he returned from Iran. Tim did not pay child support and was in arrears. He bought cars which were ultimately repossessed since he did not make the payments. He never owned a home—always rented rooms from friends. His charge accounts were maxed out and delinquent and he ultimately lost his credit. He worked as a bar tender/bouncer right after he left the military, and began drinking with his buddies after work. After a year or so, he finally got tired of being in this rut and was motivated to start a roofing business with help from family and friends. It was his first successful enterprise and we were delighted.

In the interim though, Tim showed signs of boredom and also being bi-polar. His temper flared often over inconsequential things and his relationships with all of us became strained and sporadic.

Then in August of 2002 he was arrested on a bench warrant for non-payment of child support and a DUI and was sentenced to a year at a work camp. During that time he went to Alcoholics Anonymous and promised he would never go back to his old ways again. For a while he did try hard to be rid of his past. In the meantime, though, his behavior was becoming emboldened and more aggressive. Still there were no clues that he was losing control.

He lived a double life—so well that no one, not even his roommate, knew all of his different associations. He had his family, another circle of friends in the Marines, a few acquaintances in the work camp, co-workers from his job, and workout buddies at the gym. We did not even know that he had another son in 1999 until the day of Tim's funeral. No one really knew the "inner" Tim because he hid it well.

In August of 2003, he was released from the work camp. Not even a year later he would have killed a police officer and then take his own life on July 25, 2004.

How could this have happened to a **son whom we loved so much?** He took his life and left **behind a sad mother, father, family and friends.**

*It has been over 14 years **since Tim died.** It is surreal, but it happened. In retrospect, we reexamine our life and relationship with him and think perhaps we didn't do something that was of extreme importance. Maybe we didn't give him enough support or love. But to be honest, all that happened came about for a reason—**but only God knows the reason.** Indeed, Tim was a lost soul, but in his defense, **I believe he atoned for the death of the officer by taking his own life.** I know in my heart he had a conscience and was sorry for what he did. He never contacted us or hurt anyone after that incident trying not to involve us further.*

*At his funeral, our pastor gave a hope-filled sermon, and I a heartfelt eulogy. The essence of them--**we are not our merciful God.** What we think and believe **is not how God judges us.** It is certain what **Tim did was wrong, but who is to say that his act of suicide was not his ultimate contrition.** Only God knows that.*

*As the years pass, we grieve over his loss, and the fact that his two sons will never see him. We **miss him** and his magnificence when he entered the house, smiling, joking and full of life.*

On his behalf,** he was a generous person—he never owned anything because he either lost it or gave it away. He was not materialistic. He had a big heart, was easy going and had a great sense of humor. My hope is one day I will see him again in the next life. For now, I leave this epitaph: **We love you, Tim, and may God grant you His merciful forgiveness and His everlasting peace.

With all our love, Mom, Dad, and your loving family.

Wintertime Woes

Wintertime Woes

A Short Story by Mary Minjeur

I hate *winter*. It's definitely the *snow* and my past "chilling" experiences with it that make me shudder at first glimpse. What once brought pure delight and poetry to my lips now brings words I am not permitted to repeat here.

It all began a few years ago when I took a job in the city where I live. Naturally, going back to work after being home with the kids for a few years made my driving a little rusty. But I never thought for an instant I couldn't handle it. Little did I know. Take the "minor" fender bender I had one snowy morning as I attempted to pull our mid-size Plymouth out of a parking lane at our local bank. A lovely Polish woman who couldn't speak English was driving a Volkswagen and proceeded to back into my car in spite of my frantic waving and horn blowing. I turned completely white as I watched in helpless horror the bad dream unfolding before me. It wouldn't have been so bad except I had just gotten the car out of the collision shop the previous week at a cost of $950.

Before you think I am that proverbial "woman" driver, let me explain that incident too. As I was backing the car out of the garage, I unknowingly ran over the lawn fertilizer spreader. Now this is not an easy thing to do, but it had fallen from its perch on the wall and unbeknownst to me landed just beneath the front wheel well of my car. Backing out just triggered a chain reaction with other garage inhabitants. The mauled and twisted spreader wedged itself into the demolished garbage can carrier squishing the power lawnmower which I ultimately ran over. Why I continued to keep running over everything is still beyond me. I guess I unconsciously hoped I was dreaming, or I would eventually run out of things to run over, or I didn't want the neighbors to think anything abnormal was happening and just kept going.

When I finally emerged from the garage and viewed the trail of destruction, I was totally amazed at myself—not to mention panic-stricken at the thought of telling my husband. What was I to tell him? Who'd believe such a story? Of course, the best defense is a good offense, right? So I blamed it on him. It was my contention since he drives the smaller of our two cars and has *no* obstacles on his side of the garage like the bicycles, garbage cans, lawnmower, brooms, lawn spreader, gas cans, rakes, clippers, grass catcher, toys, and miscellaneous boots, that it was obviously *his fault.* What I faintly hoped to accomplish *(to somehow diminish his wrath)* had become a reality. He was apologetic and even sympathetic, and never knew I knew about "reverse psychology." Of course, the cost of these repairs and replacement of above-mentioned items totaled $1,500 (....*and climbing.*)

Anyway, there was still more winter to come. The car of course was repaired a second time. However, I had become obsessed with having my employer or neighbors pick me up and take me to work when the weather forecast mentioned even the slightest possibility of snow just so I could avoid driving or parking. And the days I did drive, most of my fellow employees left early to avoid any possible confrontation or mishap in the parking lot. I also began to park my car so far away from the walls in our garage that suddenly our two-car garage only had room for my car. But, as justice would have it, the "*week*" passed and my confidence returned.

Alas, it was the end of February—only a few more weeks to worry. Then it happened—the biggest snowfall of the year. Foolishly I attempted to drive to work the following morning. I tried to get on the main street where traffic was moving at a snail's pace. All the while the very sight of this deluge made me tremble and shake as I awaited the inevitable.

Panic set in as I saw in my rearview mirror the angry faces of those behind me waiting for me to make that necessary left turn. All I had to do was get over that mound of snow left by the plow. I rocked the car back and forth to gain momentum, and finally the car rolled over the mound and slid out of control into the side of an oncoming car. There it was—the sound of thudding steel against steel muffled by the densely falling snow. Crunch! Same fender. I was doomed. This time the male driver furiously came out of his car stating that his car was worth so much more than mine and the time he would have to take off work to have it fixed. He had a Lincoln Continental.

I looked at my Plymouth and thought, *"Hmm. If he only knew how much more my car was going to cost—not to mention the attorney's fees for the divorce my husband was certainly going to want, he wouldn't have said that! Maybe I should have quit working since it seems to be costing me more than I am making."* Another estimate—another repair. Cost: $2,000.

Well, it's been several years since that fateful winter. Remarkably, I'm still married, and to insure the safety of the public domain, I've stopped working, since I didn't seem to be making much money anyway. My insurance rates didn't go up too much and that fender never did rust like the rest of the car. I guess the moral to this story is to quote British novelist, David Storey: *"Have confidence that if you have done a little thing well, you can do a bigger thing well too!"* Frankly, I wouldn't recommend it!

* * * * **END** * * * *

CPSIA information can be obtained
at www.ICGtesting.com
Printed in the USA
FFHW02n1922270818
48004595-51706FF